found

This is a Magabala Book
Leading Publisher of Aboriginal and Torres Strait Islander Storytellers.
Changing the World, One Story at a Time.

First published 2020, reprinted 2023
Magabala Books Aboriginal Corporation
1 Bagot Rd, Broome Western Australia
www.magabala.com e: sales@magabala.com

Magabala Books is assisted by the Australian Government through Creative Australia, its principal arts investment and advisory body. The State of Western Australia has made an investment in this project through the Department of Local Government, Sport and Cultural Industries.

Magabala Books is Australia's only independent Aboriginal and Torres Strait Islander publishing house. Magabala Books acknowledges the Traditional Owners of the Country on which we live and work. We recognise the unbroken connection to traditional lands, waters and cultures. Through what we publish, we honour all our Elders, peoples and stories, past, present and future.

Editing, cover and internal design by Cathie Tasker & Deborah Brown
Printed in China by 1010 Printing International

Cataloguing-in-publication data available from the National Library of Australia

ISBN 978-1-925936-48-3

A catalogue record for this book is available from the National Library of Australia

Department of Local Government, Sport and Cultural Industries
Australian Government
Creative Australia

found

Bruce Pascoe

illustrated by
Charmaine Ledden-Lewis

I'm all alone.

I want my **mother**
and **sisters**
and **brothers.**

But they're all GONE.

I can see some **horses**

and some **wood ducks**...

And a **man**.

The man pushed us all into the back of a truck.

I **jumped** and **flew** through the air...

and **ran**.

The man had **stolen** my mother.

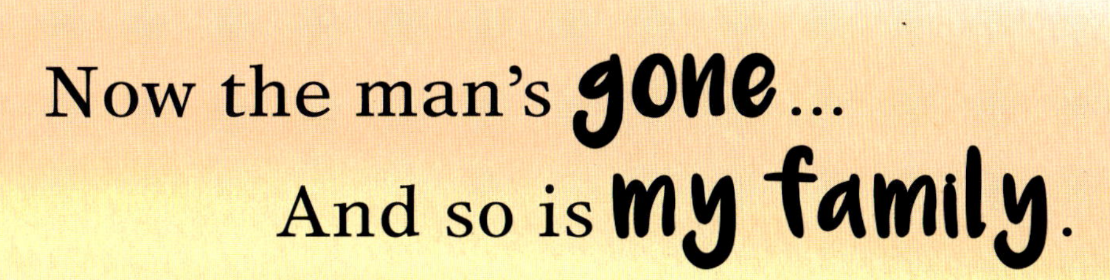

Now the man's **gone**...
And so is **my family**.

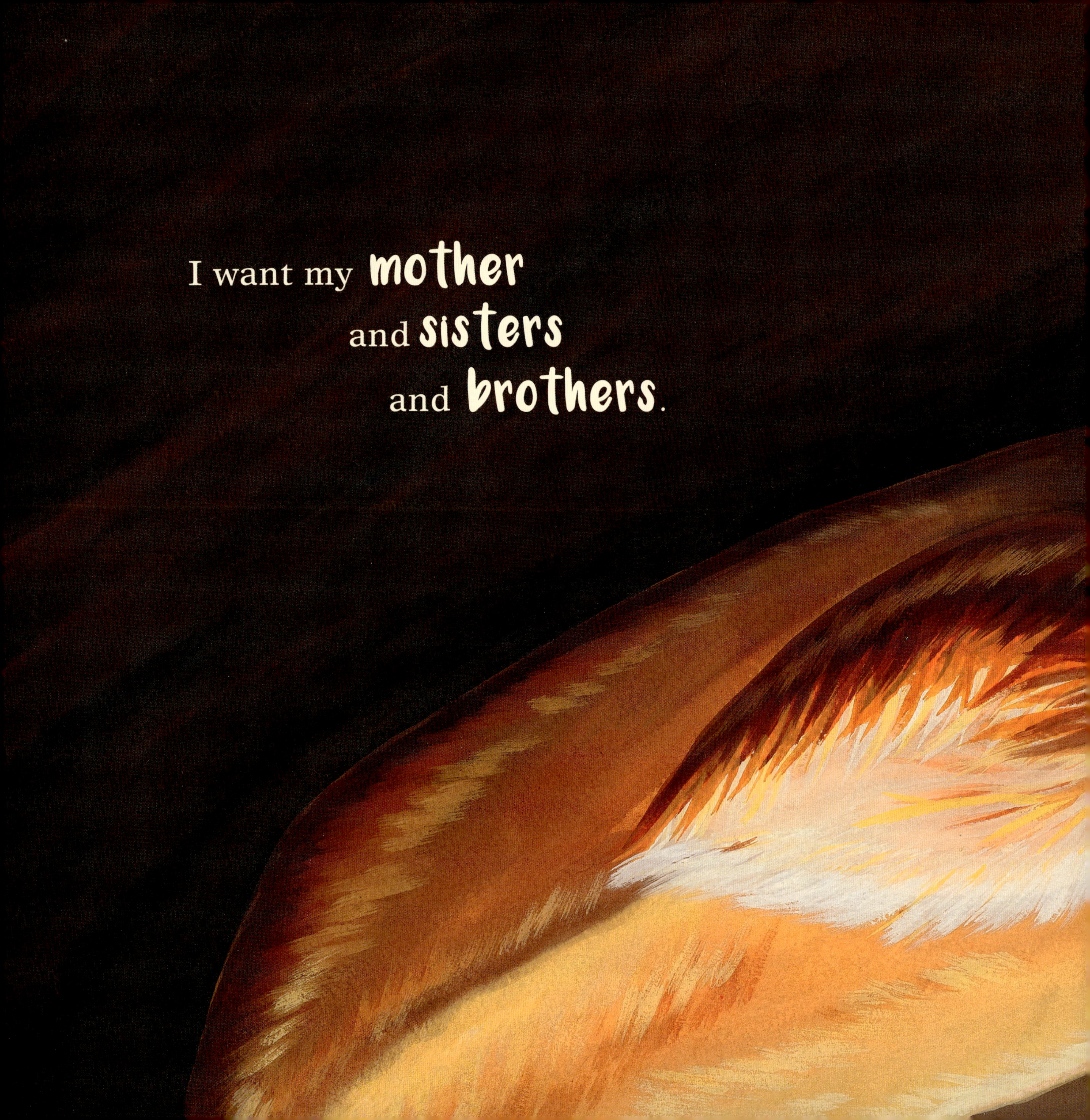
I want my mother
and sisters
and brothers.

I'm **all alone.**

I run to the river.

I can see some horses.
They're **not** my family,
but they're here.

I go over to them.

They're **not** my family,

but they have **hooves** and **fur.**

I hear **someone**.

I charge down the hill
but I don't **see** my family.

I can hear **my mother**.

Mooo oooo

I call out for her
Mo

and she calls out for me.

MoOOOo oooo

I hear her over the river.

oooooo

I see **my mother**.

She calls out for me again.

I race over
the river
and she
trots up.

She smells my breath
and licks my neck...

I have **found** my mother.

Now I am **home**...

with **my family.**

Bruce Pascoe

Bruce Pascoe has published widely in both adult and young adult literature and has won numerous awards including the New South Wales Premier's Book of the Year Award in 2016 for *Dark Emu* and the Prime Minister's Literature Award for Young Adult fiction for *Fog, a dox* in 2013. In 2018 he was awarded the Australia Council Award for Lifetime Achievement in Literature. Bruce is a born storyteller and this is his first children's picture book. Bruce is a Yuin, Bunurong and Tasmanian man. He has enjoyed watching the progress of Charmaine's artwork and is excited by the result.

Charmaine Ledden-Lewis

Charmaine is a Blue Mountains artist, and descendant of the Bundjalung people. Her matriarchal lineage is a living legacy of the stolen generation. She is a vocal advocate for people like herself who have had their history and opportunity to culture stolen from them.

Raised in a loving family surrounded by art and music, Charmaine developed a passion for all things creative from an early age, and strives to provide such an environment for her two sons, taking great pleasure in nurturing creativity with them. Further, she believes we are all artists and encourages everyone to transcend inhibition and find their creative expression!

Magabala Books is Australia's leading Indigenous publisher. Aboriginal owned and controlled, Magabala celebrated thirty years of publishing in 2017. Based in Broome, Western Australia, Magabala is a national publishing house and its award-winning books include children's picture books, junior and young adult fiction, adult fiction, memoir, non-fiction and poetry. Magabala is renowned for its program of professional development of Aboriginal and Torres Strait Islander authors and illustrators, and its commitment to supporting storytellers to share their stories with the world.

THE KESTIN INDIGENOUS ILLUSTRATOR AWARD

Charmaine is the winner of Magabala's second Kestin Indigenous Illustrator Award. The aim of the Award is to mentor new and emerging Indigenous illustrators, or artists with an interest in becoming illustrators, in the production of illustrations for a children's picture book to be published by Magabala. The award is funded by the Kestin Family Foundation.